THE THUMB
IN THE BOX

THE THUMB IN THE BOX

Ken Roberts

•

ILLUSTRATED BY

Leanne Franson

A Groundwood Book

DOUGLAS & McINTYRE
TORONTO VANCOUVER BUFFALO

Groundwood Books/Douglas & McIntyre
720 Bathurst Street, Suite 500, Toronto, Ontario M5S 2R4

Distributed in the USA by Publishers Group West
1700 Fourth Street, Berkeley, CA 94710

We acknowledge the financial support of the Canada Council for
the Arts, the Ontario Arts Council and the Government of
Canada through the Book Publishing Industry Development
Program for our publishing activities.

ONTARIO ARTS COUNCIL
CONSEIL DES ARTS DE L'ONTARIO

Canadian Cataloguing in Publication Data
Roberts, Ken, 1946-
The thumb in the box
1st ed.
"A Groundwood book".
ISBN 0-88899-421-4 (bound) ISBN 0-88899-422-2 (pbk.)
I. Franson, Leanne. II. Title.
PS8585.O2968T48 2001   jC813'.54   C00-932361-9
PZ7.R62Th 2001

Printed and bound in Canada

To Caleb and Zoë,
with love.

Contents

1
THE FIRE

T HIS is a story about a fire truck being driven into the ocean and two people taking off their thumbs. Don't worry, though. Nobody gets hurt.

The village of New Auckland is on the coast of British Columbia. It is north of Prince Rupert and south of Linda Evers Mountain, a round mountain with a cliff on the south side. At the base of the cliff a narrow channel leads into a bay called Pirate's Inlet. New Auckland is just behind the mountain, tucked onto a crescent-shaped beach.

Two rows of small wooden houses line the beach. Cedar sidewalks connect the houses, and the sidewalks are old and gray. The largest two buildings are the community center and the six-room school.

On the night of the fire that starts this story, I was eleven years old, walking slowly along the wooden sidewalk closest to the water. I remember looking down at the planks, staring at every loose nail and clump of moss. I was probably grinning. People say I grinned all the time, like I had a secret.

My name was, as it is still, Leon Mazzei, but I had better not describe my village or me right now. The smoke has reached Muriel, and she has roared.

Muriel the lion was once a pet owned by a woman who sneaked her onto a cruise ship sailing to Alaska.

Muriel wasn't much more than a cub at the time. The crew found her, and the captain, who had lost an arm to a lion when he pointed out a jeep window in Africa, turned his ship into Pirate's Inlet and dropped anchor just off the beach in front of our village. The captain blew the ship's deep-pitched whistle to make sure people in New Auckland noticed his vessel. He didn't need to blow the whistle at all. Half the village was standing on the shore, staring in surprise.

A small boat was lowered, and three crew members motored over to the dock. They left the lion cub, promising to let authorities in Prince Rupert know it was there. Maybe they did, but nobody ever came and Muriel became the village pet. She lived, as she does still, in a huge pen behind the community center.

On the night of the fire, I lifted my head, wondering why Muriel was roaring. She usually roared early in the morning, when she was hungry.

"Fire!" I yelled as soon as I spotted the smoke rising from behind Mrs. Yatulis's house. Doors opened, and people ran out carrying buckets.

"The Yatulis shed," I yelled, pointing.

Buckets of ocean water were passed, hand to hand, and thrown onto the fire. I stood in the children's line, quickly passing the empty buckets back down to the water's edge.

We were all nervous. We knew that if it looked as if the fire was going to leap toward another building, then the houses around the fire would be torn down fast so the whole village didn't burn.

We didn't talk, not until the fire was almost out. After the whistle was blown, telling us to stop, my best friend Susan and I ran to see the last of the blaze.

"We've got to do something," shouted our mayor, Charlie Semanov, silhouetted in front of the dying fire. Charlie was tall and wide and had wild, uncombed hair and a frizzy gray beard. He had a deep voice, too.

"What if this fire had started when the boats were out and half of us were fishing? The whole village could have burned," yelled Charlie. "We need a big saltwater pump so that we can shoot lots of water right onto a fire without a bucket line."

People cheered and, the next morning, as the ashes of the shed still smoldered, Charlie wrote to the Government of Canada.

Curtis Vandermeulen, Member of Parliament for the Northwest Coast, wrote back and said he was proud to promise that the Canadian government could send an entire fire truck to New Auckland.

"We don't need a fire truck," Charlie wrote. "We just need a water pump. Our entire village is only as long as a couple of football fields. We don't even have a road."

"A town without a road!" wrote Mr. Vandermeulen. "The Canadian government will send money for a sandy road and for a small fire station, too. You'll have to hire somebody to build the fire station. I've already ordered the fire truck and it comes with two ladders, four axes, one hundred meters of canvas hose and a saltwater pump."

"Oh, well," thought Mayor Charlie. "At least we'll get our pump."

Charlie gave the job of building the fire station to his son, who was also named Charlie. Little Charlie lived in Vancouver, so he had to come back to the village.

Little Charlie is the one who showed me how to take off my thumb.

You'll see.

2
LITTLE CHARLIE'S THUMB

THE morning after Little Charlie came back, I heard people laughing over at the dock. I ran over as fast as I could.

My dad was there. Dad was a tall man, completely bald and a little afraid of getting skin cancer on top of his head. He liked New Auckland because there was hardly any sun. Even when the sun was shining, it could only sneak between the towering mountains for a couple of hours in the middle of the day.

"What's going on?" I yelled from the foot of the dock.

"Nothing you can see," said Dad. "It's too gross."

"Let him see," whispered Big Charlie. "This could be great."

"What can't I see?" I asked, stopping in front of Dad. "And if it's so gross, why was Little Charlie laughing?"

I didn't have to ask who had been laughing. I knew it was Little Charlie. Nobody talked or laughed as loudly as a Semanov, and Little Charlie was the loudest Semanov of all.

Whenever Charlie Semanov's son came home, everyone called the father Big Charlie and the son Little Charlie, even though Little Charlie was bigger than his dad and his dad wasn't small at all. Little Charlie looked like an upright bear. He was hairy and threw his weight from side to side as he ambled along.

"Little Charlie was laughing at me," said Dad. "Little Charlie's thumb was cut off when he was working on a construction project in Vancouver. He showed it to me and I got sick to my stomach. Little Charlie thought that was funny."

"But I can see both his thumbs," I said.

"The doctors reattached it," said Little Charlie, holding up his right thumb.

"So what?" I asked. "That's not gross. My dad got sick looking at a thumb?"

"I can take my thumb off," said Little Charlie quietly. "My thumb and I were rushed to a hospital, where doctors stuffed it, drilled two little holes in each side and pushed tiny flesh-colored screws in place. I can take my thumb off and show it to you if you want."

"Hey, Little Charlie," said Dad, shaking his head. "I don't think so."

"Dad!" I exclaimed. "I can handle it."

"He is getting pretty big," said Little Charlie. "I barely recognized you, Leon."

"Dad?" I pleaded.

"I suppose it's all right."

"Yeah!" I exclaimed.

Little Charlie reached into his pocket, pulled out a small screwdriver, turned his back for privacy and removed each screw. Carefully, Little Charlie put the screws back into his pocket and pulled out a cardboard jewelry case with cotton on the bottom. He dropped the severed tip of his thumb on top of the cotton, faced me and stretched out the box so I could see.

"I have to take it off at night," said Little Charlie.

I stepped forward and looked inside. The thumb lay on a wad of cotton. I stared at the hair below the knuckle and wondered if the hair was real or fake. Could hair grow on a thumb that had been severed and stuffed and screwed back in place?

I stared at the spot where the thumb seemed to disappear down inside the cotton. I figured that Little Charlie had tucked the severed end of the thumb into the cotton, not wanting anyone to see that part.

It must be embarrassing, I thought,

still staring at the thumb. I looked at the thumbnail and at the skin around it, noticing that some of the skin had been picked, like Dad sometimes did to his real thumb. I frowned, wondering if the skin had looked that way when the doctors fixed it or if the skin still grew and Little Charlie could still chew at the skin of his severed thumb. If he could, what would keep him from chewing the skin off his entire thumb?

The thumb wiggled.

I yelled and stepped back fast, almost running. My feet moved so quickly that I backed right off the side of the dock.

The water in Pirate's Inlet is cold, and the moment my feet touched the water, I figured out the joke.

Little Charlie Semanov had not lost

his thumb working in construction. The thumb in the box was his own, still attached and still working. There was a hole in the bottom of that cardboard jewelry box, and there was a hole in the cotton, too. When Little Charlie's back was turned and nobody could see, Little Charlie slipped his perfectly good thumb into the bottom of the jewelry case, pressing his thumb flat against the cotton.

I was laughing when my head went under and laughing even harder when I came back up and reached for the arms stretched out to me.

As Little Charlie reached down and pulled me from the water, I could hardly wait until he wiggled his thumb for Susan. I threw back my head and laughed again.

3
SUSAN

SUSAN was six months younger than me, and I was her only friend. Susan could have made a fortune on a TV game show. She knew who had won the Stanley Cup each year for decades, even though she didn't like sports. She knew the distances between planets, the life expectancies of frogs and slugs, and the differences between types of roses, even though there were no roses in New Auckland.

People, especially adults, found themselves getting mad at Susan when all she ever seemed to do was to know facts that were right. Whenever Susan did state a fact, somebody almost always said she was wrong, hoping that she was wrong but not really knowing why she might be wrong.

I knew something about Susan that most people didn't. I knew that even though Susan was a genius when it came to facts, she could always be fooled by something that wasn't in a book. She was gullible.

I found Susan up on Linda Evers Mountain. There was a small spring up there. The village water came from the spring. Sometimes Susan and I liked to climb up to the spring, where we could catch a glimpse of the ocean.

"Little Charlie can take off his thumb," I said, running up the trail. "He showed me this morning. You were probably still asleep. The doctors took out all the veins in the part of the thumb that they attached. They stuffed it with something like foam. Little Charlie's thumb looks real and the bone is the same and the skin is the same because it was preserved with some special type of medicine or something. But Little Charlie can't feel anything in that thumb."

"Where is Little Charlie?" asked Susan. "Let's go find him."

"I think he's working on the fire station," I said casually. Susan couldn't tell that I was grinning even more than usual, since my usual grin is huge.

"Let's go right now," said Susan, hitching up her pants and starting to run.

Little Charlie was wearing construction boots and blue jeans. It was a hot day. He wasn't wearing a shirt. His wide tool belt, with leather pouches for nails and screws, rested on the ground.

Annie Pritchard and Mrs. Yatulis were sitting in the shade of Annie's house, holding cardboard signs that said, "No Fire Truck! No Road!"

It is time to say a bit about Annie Pritchard, since she's in this story a lot.

During the summer of the fire truck, Annie was seventy-seven years old. She walked slowly, leaning heavily on a walking stick that one of her grandchildren had carved for her. Annie lived up near the church, in the same small house where she was born.

Annie didn't have to live there. She was rich. Her art, mostly paintings of trees seen through fog, were displayed in art galleries around the world.

Annie dressed like almost everyone else in New Auckland, except she wore a lot of silver bracelets and rings, all engraved by Northwest Coast artists. Some people said Annie could walk a lot taller if she wasn't weighed down by so much jewelry.

Annie Pritchard paid for the new community center and basketball court. When the construction crew had finished laying the hardwood basketball court, and before they varnished it, Annie painted the center court jump circle. She had worked out the design.

It was a picture of the entire village as seen through the eye of a soaring raven. Annie Pritchard had never flown over the village, although the pilot who delivered groceries every Thursday offered to take her up when he heard what she was planning to paint. She turned him down.

"I'd rather imagine it," she said softly, patting the pilot's arm.

The bleachers were full on the night the community center officially opened, a game that featured the New Auckland Cohos against the Bella Bella Sockeyes. Every resident of New Auckland was crammed into the home-side stands. Half of Bella Bella was crowded into the stands facing them.

The Bella Bella basketball fans had to share their benches with art critics from Vancouver and Toronto and New York and San Francisco and even one from Paris. The art critics had come to see the largest painting Annie Pritchard ever created—the basketball jump circle in the middle of the floor. They came to watch basketball players dribble on the painting and sweat on the painting and fall on the painting and skid across the painting. They groaned and shut their eyes every time a player ran across center court.

The painting was, they all agreed, the best work Annie Pritchard had ever produced. It was, they all agreed and eventually wrote in their newspapers and magazines, worth more than the entire community center Annie Pritchard had donated to the village she loved.

"You don't want a fire truck?" I asked Annie.

"No," Annie said. "I'm glad to see Little Charlie and everything, but when I visit big cities, I love telling people that there are no roads in my town, no cars and no trucks of any kind. I won't be able to say that any more. We're going to have a truck."

"Yeah," said Mrs. Yatulis. "I've lived in cities and towns with trucks and cars. You have to build fences to keep kids off the street so they won't get hurt. Besides, the smog is awful."

"But we'll have just one fire truck," said Susan. "There won't be much smog. The truck will only move a few hundred meters a year. There won't be much traffic, either."

"But we'll have to keep that road clear," insisted Annie, "and there's precious little space in town right now. We don't need a road. We need a park, with playground equipment."

"It's just a sand road," I said, smiling. "There won't be painted lines down the middle or anything. We can play right on the sand."

"Now there's a good habit to encourage in young people," muttered Mrs. Yatulis, throwing her arms up high. "First we get ourselves a truck and now these children are talking about playing on the road as if it's perfectly normal."

Susan pulled on my sleeve, glancing toward Little Charlie, who was digging foundation holes.

"Can we get you anything, Little Charlie?" Susan asked. She didn't want to talk about the thumb right away.

"No, thanks," said Little Charlie, concentrating on his work.

"I told Susan that you showed me your thumb this morning," I said. "She wants to see it, too."

Little Charlie stopped digging for a moment and looked at us. He put down his shovel and pulled off his work gloves. He squeezed his work gloves under one arm so they wouldn't fall and then held up his right hand, pointing to his thumb.

"There," said Little Charlie, showing the thumb to Susan. Little Charlie started to put his gloves back on. "Now you've seen my thumb."

"Could you, uh, take it off for me?" asked Susan. "I've never seen anybody take off a thumb."

Little Charlie shook his head.

"Sorry," he said. "Not while I'm working. The more I tighten the screws the harder I can squeeze my thumb. But I need just the right pressure when I'm working and it takes me about thirty minutes to make the adjustments. If I don't do it right, then I might not grip the hammer tightly enough and it might fly out of my hand and hurt somebody. So I can't take my thumb off. Not right now."

"Oh," said Susan.

I was surprised. I wanted Little Charlie to take off his thumb so I could watch Susan scream.

Little Charlie finished slipping his hand back inside his work glove, picked up his shovel and scooped several loads of dirt.

Susan and I stared at each other for a moment and then turned to leave, disappointed.

"But, you know," said Little Charlie, still working. "I'm not going to be wearing these gloves much longer because I don't like to wear gloves when I hammer. Sometimes, if the adjustment is too loose, my thumb can fall off. Once it flew right over my shoulder. I was watching the hammer at the time so I didn't see where the thumb landed. It took me three hours to find it. Most people can't lose their thumbs, of course, because their thumbs are connected to the rest of their bodies, but I can. So it would help me if you could stick around and keep an eye on my right thumb. If you help, I'll take off my thumb after work."

Susan and I sat and watched, taking turns. It wasn't too hard. We only had to watch really hard when Little Charlie took a swing with his hammer. The rest of the time his thumb wasn't going to fly too far if it did come off. I had to watch as closely as Susan so she wouldn't get suspicious.

My dad brought us lunch.

By the end of the day, Little Charlie had poured concrete into each of the foundation holes. He had also cut and nailed together some of the ceiling joists. They were stacked against the cliff at the bottom of Linda Evers Mountain, ready to be raised into place when needed.

"Well," said Little Charlie, picking up his tool belt and circular saw. "I guess that's about it for the day." He stretched his back.

Susan didn't find it odd that a crowd was gathering. The fire station was the most exciting thing to happen in New Auckland since the community center opened.

"Looks good," said Big Charlie, peering down at one of the concrete support holes.

Dad hit a couple of the joists with the palm of his hand and nodded.

Dad and I weren't from New Auckland. Dad had been raised in Toronto and had worked as a teacher in Vancouver. I was born in Vancouver. After Mom died, the Prince Rupert School District offered Dad a job as principal but didn't tell him the school was in a tiny little fishing village with no cars and no streets and no stores.

Dad accepted, but when he saw New Auckland he would have run away if there had been any place to go or any way to get there.

After a year, he never left, not even during the summer months when there was no school. Everyone knew he was from the city, though. Dad wore a tie every day. He ironed his shirts, too. Dad owned the only iron in New Auckland.

"Thanks for keeping an eye on my thumb," said Little Charlie, turning to Susan and me.

"That's all right," said Susan.

"Do you want me to take it off for you now?" Little Charlie asked casually.

"Sure," said Susan and I together, both grinning but for different reasons.

Little Charlie reached into his back pocket and pulled out his cardboard box and his screwdriver. Then he turned around and slipped his finger through the hole in the bottom of the box. He twisted his neck and winked at

Susan and me, pocketing the screw-driver. He turned around to face us, holding out the box, the lid raised.

"There," said Little Charlie. "My thumb."

Susan and I ran up to Little Charlie and bent down to look at the severed thumb. Susan didn't mind the crowd.

We stared down at the box and even though I knew the joke, I still flinched when it wiggled. Susan stood still, her eyes closed tightly, and she screamed. I don't know why I found it so funny that my best friend was screaming, but I sure did.

By the end of the week I'd seen Little Charlie show his thumb to another twenty-eight people in the village, two visiting fishermen, the pilot of the seaplane, three families in sailboats and a visiting relative, who wasn't much fun because she knew the joke. I laughed every time but never as hard as when Susan screamed.

4
THE FIRE
TRUCK

ON the morning the fire truck was due to arrive, I got up and put on my best pants, a white shirt, good shoes and my only tie. The tie was dark blue with small red sailboats crisscrossing up and down and back and forth. Some of the boats seemed to sail around the edge of the tie.

"Why are you so dressed up?" asked Dad.

"The fire truck," I said calmly, sitting down at the kitchen table with my bowl of cereal. "It's coming today."

"You do realize that this fire truck won't know you're wearing a tie."

"Yes, Dad. I know we are not greeting Tommy the Talking Fire Truck."

"So why the tie?"

"I don't know. Not much happens around here most days. Today we're getting a fire truck, the first truck or car in any direction for maybe fifty kilometers. Besides," I added, taking my first spoonful of cereal, "you're wearing a tie."

"I wear a tie every day. If we both wear ties then we might look like father and son idiots. We'll be the only ones in the entire village with ties."

"No, we won't. I heard Little Charlie and his dad say they are going to wear ties today."

"They are?"

"Yeah."

"I didn't know they owned ties."

"Well, I guess they do."

Two hundred eighteen people were waiting on the beach staring out into the inlet at Big Charlie Semanov's boat. Most of the men wore ties. Big Charlie, standing at the prow of his boat, wasn't staring back. He was gazing out at the ocean.

The moment the tugboat rounded Newman's Point, Big Charlie would blow his whistle. It was important that the tugboat be in perfect position at least two hours before low tide.

The tug was supposed to push the barge it was towing close to shore while the water was high. Then the tug was going to back away and let the tide ebb, stranding the barge on wet sand.

The whistle on Big Charlie's boat blew long and hard, echoing off the mountains so much that it sounded as if the inlet was full of boats. I started to jump up and down, laughing.

"Hey, Leon," said Little Charlie, "calm down. It'll be awhile."

"The fire station looks great," I told Little Charlie.

"It looks all right," said Little Charlie. "I'm usually all thumbs," he added with a chuckle. "Come on. Let's greet this fire truck."

The dock was full of people, all getting on boats so they could ride out to a spot where they could peer between the mountains toward the ocean and greet the tug.

Little Charlie and I hopped onto Annie Pritchard's boat.

"Welcome aboard," shouted Annie. Most mornings she used her boat to drift around Pirate's Inlet picking sites to paint. The boat was wooden and the wood was sanded and varnished.

Little Charlie slipped the rope from a cleat on the dock. The engine sputtered to a start, and Annie slowly followed other boats out into the inlet.

"You need a new engine," said Little Charlie, listening.

"I know. Your dad has been telling me the same thing. I'm an artist, remember? Not a mechanic."

"Any mechanic who can fix this old engine would have to be a creative genius, too," said Little Charlie. "Like I said, you need a new engine."

"You going to get me an engine?" asked Annie with a wink.

"I think we all should," said Little Charlie, grinning. "Right, Leon?"

"Right," I replied. "Soon, too," I added, climbing onto the top of the small cabin, where the wind seemed to blow stronger and the smell of salt and seaweed was strong. Annie slowed down, rocking gently beside the other boats.

We bobbed quietly, watching the gap between the mountains, the ocean visible all the way to the horizon. It was a sight that always stunned me. I was used to the tiny world of Pirate's Inlet where the sky was small.

"There!" shouted Little Charlie, pointing.

I squinted and spotted the tugboat. A long black cable trailed behind it. A barge was connected to the cable. A tarp-covered mound rested on top of the barge, and a man was scurrying around the edges of the mound, untying ropes. He ran to the front of the barge and pulled on a long rope. The black canvas tarp that covered the fire truck flew up and flapped in the wind like a gigantic pirate's flag.

The fire truck was redder and brighter than any fire or sunset I had ever seen. It was beautiful.

The man on the boat let go of the tarp, and it fell behind the truck. Villagers cheered. The tugboat and the barge slowly turned into Pirate's Inlet. The fishing fleet greeted it with bells and whistles and horns.

The man on the barge climbed into the fire truck, and the fire truck answered the welcoming chorus with a sound of its own.

"A siren," shouted Little Charlie,

laughing. "The fire truck has a siren."

"Cool," I said.

The tugboat pulled the barge close to the beach and then, after a crew member disconnected the cable, nudged the barge still closer.

"Who's that man standing beside the fire truck?" I asked Annie.

"I think that's our Member of Parliament," said Annie. "Nobody else would wave so much. Politicians are awfully friendly."

The man on the barge threw the anchor overboard so the barge wouldn't drift away. He waved to Big Charlie and then reached into the fire truck and pulled out a fireman's helmet. He waved it for people on the boats to see.

"Good morning," he shouted through a megaphone. "I am your

Member of Parliament, Curtis Vander-meulen, and here is the fire truck I promised. I always keep my promises."

Big Charlie pulled up to the back of the barge and tied his boat alongside. When the tide went out, there would still be enough water behind the barge to keep Big Charlie's fishing boat afloat.

Big Charlie hopped onto the barge and shook Mr. Vandermeulen's hand.

Annie slowly brought her boat alongside the barge, and Little Charlie jumped onto it, too.

"What do we do now?" I asked.

"Wait," said Annie.

Annie dropped anchor and sat at the back of her boat, eating potato chips and sipping Coke while we waited for the tide to drop.

Up on the barge, Curtis Vandermeulen shook hands with both Charlies and patted the fire truck.

"I was in Prince Rupert," said Curtis Vandermeulen. "I spotted the fire truck down at the docks and decided to ride out with it."

Curtis Vandermeulen was a thin man with thick, long dark hair that flapped in the wind.

"Glad you could make it," said Big Charlie. "We've got a big day planned."

"How are we going to get the fire truck on shore?" asked Curtis Vandermeulen.

Big Charlie and Little Charlie took turns explaining how they would wait for the tide to fall and then pull down the long steel ramp at the beach end of the barge and drive the fire truck onto the wet sand.

"That fire truck looks awfully heavy," said Mr. Vandermeulen, trying to control his hair with one hand while he talked.

"It does," agreed Little Charlie, nodding. "Awfully heavy."

"The mud under that barge will be soft," said Curtis Vandermeulen, peering over the side of the barge.

"Awfully soft," agreed Big Charlie.

"I remember once," said Curtis Vandermeulen, still looking over the side, "when I was about ten years old and I walked out into the muck down by Campbell River during a low tide. I wanted to get a ball that had fallen off my parents' boat. I sank down to my knees. When my parents pulled me out, my boots slipped off. Those boots are still down there someplace. I only weighed about thirty kilos and I got stuck. This truck weighs thousands of kilos, so how is it going to ride along on top of all that mud?"

"Little Charlie and our local school principal worked it out," said Big Charlie. "That's why all the logs are stacked up on shore," he added, pointing to the beach. "We're going to put logs in front of the wheels as the truck inches toward the beach. The logs will spread the weight of the fire truck over a larger area."

"It still doesn't look like it will work."

"No," said Big Charlie, looking over the side of the barge. "It doesn't."

"Could that fire truck sink so far

that it would disappear under the mud?" asked Curtis Vandermeulen.

"No," said Big Charlie. "I'm sure it couldn't. There's probably a bottom. I don't think that truck could sink more than a meter. Maximum."

"Will it?" asked Mr. Vandermeulen, looking up at Big Charlie and then waving toward all the boats.

Big Charlie shrugged. "I guess that's part of the drama," he said slowly, looking his Member of Parliament in the eye. "I guess that's what we're all waiting to see. Some people are hoping it will sink."

"Why?" asked Mr. Vandermeulen, stunned.

"There has never been any motor vehicle in New Auckland. Not permanently. There was a tractor here to help with the construction of the community center, but the tractor's gone now. Some people live here at least partly because they don't like cars and trucks. They're worried that this fire truck is just the start, as if we'll have freeways and traffic jams within a year."

"But you need that pump, right?"

"Sure," said Big Charlie. "We need that pump. But pumps only cost a few thousand dollars. It cost more money than that to build the fire station and make a road for this truck. We've got to keep that road ready for the truck, too, and that's valuable land, at least to us."

I didn't hear any more of their talk. Annie Pritchard lifted anchor and pulled her boat back so it wouldn't get stuck. Her boat rode lower in the water than Big Charlie's.

Annie and I stared at the barge. The end closest to the beach was gently resting on the bottom.

"It'll be at least a half hour still," said Annie. "We've got plenty of time. That politician is probably a nice man but he's mighty proud of himself, isn't he?"

"Sure," I said. "Maybe he feels he has a right to be proud. He did get us a fire engine."

"Not that we need one," muttered Annie. "I guess I just don't like to see so much pride. He didn't build that fire engine. He just brought it here."

"You build things," I said. "You make paintings. So you have a right to be a really proud person, right?"

"Hmm. I'll tell you a secret I've never told anybody else, ever. Okay, Leon?"

"Sure," I said. "What?"

"You know I'm famous, right?"

"Right," I said, nodding.

"Famous means that people recognize you or at least know who you are. We all know each other in New Auckland so we're all sort of famous here. But I'm famous in the rest of the world, too. People know who I am and they pay a lot of money for my paintings, right?"

"Yeah," I said.

"Well, when I go out into the world to accept a prize or open a show some place, it would be easy for me to get pretty full of myself, to puff up with pride. There's nothing wrong with pride, not at all, and it's wonderful to know that people like my paintings, but there is a chance that I could begin to feel that I'm something special. Famous is all right. Special is wrong. There is something wrong with feeling you're better than others. So, when I venture out into the world, I do something before I go."

"What?" I asked.

"Do I look like the type of person who would paint her toenails bright pink?"

"No," I said, laughing. "Of course not."

"Well, I do. I paint them the night before I fly out to give lectures or accept awards."

"But...why?"

"Because I think it's silly for an old woman to paint her toenails. When people tell me I'm wonderful and special, I just think of the fact that inside my shoes I have pink toenails and it makes me feel so silly that I don't get too puffed up with pride."

I shivered, thinking of Annie Pritchard, who was old enough to have wrinkles on her toenails, sitting down and painting those toenails a bright pink.

"Where do you get the nail polish?" I asked after a while.

"I buy it when I go to one of those cities. It's a shade called Flamingo."

"Why tell me?"

"I don't know. We're waiting. We're talking. Maybe I'm afraid that some day—hopefully not too soon—I'll die and people will find me and my old toenails will be painted pink and people will think I was a crazy old coot. You can tell them I wasn't crazy. You can tell them I just didn't want to be special."

5
A FIRE TRUCK RIDE

BIG Charlie and Curtis Vandermeulen sat talking and laughing and tossing sunflower seed shells out the window of the fire truck. Every few minutes, Big Charlie got out and peered over the side, checking the water level.

When the barge was almost surrounded by wet sand and pebbles, Big Charlie leaned back into the truck and said something to Mr. Vandermeulen. Mr. Vandermeulen opened the passenger door, hopped out and looked over the side. Big Charlie helped him onto the back of the truck, facing the line of fishing boats. Big Charlie handed the Member of Parliament his megaphone.

"Here's your fire truck," said our Member of Parliament.

We cheered.

"And now," said Mr. Vandermeulen, "I hand the keys to your mayor and my new friend, Charlie Semanov."

Mr. Vandermeulen reached into his pocket. Big Charlie climbed onto the truck and Mr. Vandermeulen handed him the keys. Big Charlie took the keys and put them into his pocket.

"It's ours?" asked Big Charlie, leaning toward the megaphone.

"Yes," said the Member of Parliament. "It's all yours."

"To keep?"

"To keep," said Mr. Vandermeulen, grinning and nodding.

"And we can do what we want with it?" asked Big Charlie.

Annie and I looked at each other and smiled, even though she didn't want a fire truck at all.

"Within reason," said the MP, laughing. "You've read the contract. You can't sell it."

I looked at Annie.

"We won't sell it, will we, Annie?" I said.

"No, we won't," said Annie. "We won't sell it. No need to sell it."

A raven settled on the fire truck's hood, like an ornament. Big Charlie took the keys out of his pocket and waved them at the gathered boats. Big Charlie hopped inside the cab and turned on the engine, reaching up to push a button so the fire truck's siren would scream. The raven squawked, flapped its wings and flew up into the sky, circling and watching. Behind the gym, Muriel roared.

"What was that?" asked Curtis Vandermeulen, glancing up at the mountains.

"It was a lion," said Big Charlie casually.

"A mountain lion?"

"No. One of those African lions with the hairy necklace, like in the movies."

"You're kidding, right?"

"No. There's a real lion here."

Big Charlie didn't bother to tell Mr. Vandermeulen that the lion was tame and sitting in a cage. He didn't tell him that our lion was female and didn't have a mane. It was more fun to watch the Member of Parliament frown and search the mountains.

Little Charlie and the tugboat operator turned the huge handles at each side of the front of the barge. A metal ramp was slowly lowered toward the wet, rocky surface of New Auckland's low tide beach. The ramp came to a rest fifty meters from the dry sand.

On shore, men and women rolled logs down the beach toward the bottom of the barge's ramp. They pushed the logs into place, creating a rough road.

Big Charlie put the fire truck's engine in gear. Without thinking, I jumped over the side of Annie's boat into the waist-high water, and I ran toward the barge.

"What are you doing?" yelled Annie.

"This may be my only chance to ride a fire truck," I yelled back.

I climbed a ladder on the side of the barge and hopped onto the back of the fire truck where the firefighters ride. Big Charlie slowly drove the truck down the ramp. The front wheels touched the logs and pushed them deeper into the wet sand.

Big Charlie edged the truck forward until it rested completely on the logs. The truck slowly moved over the half-sunken logs.

The front wheels of the truck suddenly slipped between two logs. Big Charlie gunned the fire truck's engine and the front wheels dug deeper into the sand. The back wheels spit out logs and began to spin.

The fire truck was stuck, but Big

Charlie kept gunning the engine, digging the wheels deeper into the wet sand.

Curtis Vandermeulen rushed up to the cab and leaned into the window.

"Stop," he yelled to Big Charlie. "You're making it worse. Stop spinning the wheels."

Big Charlie turned off the engine and hopped out of the cab. He slowly strolled toward the front of the fire truck and peered at the wheels. He took off his hat and scratched his head.

"Well, how about that," he said to Curtis Vandermeulen.

"Why did you keep spinning your wheels?" yelled our Member of Parliament.

"Hey," said Big Charlie calmly. "I don't know much about driving. I haven't even got my driver's licence."

"What?"

"I've never needed to drive anything but a boat."

"Can we pull it out?" asked our Member of Parliament. "You know, with a winch or something."

"Sure," said Big Charlie. "Good idea. But I think this fire truck weighs too much. We'll have to lighten it. And we'll have to work fast. In an hour the water will be up past the tops of the wheels. Hey, if this truck rusts, can you get us another one?"

"No," shouted Curtis Vandermeulen. "You took possession. You're responsible. It's your truck."

"Good," said Big Charlie, grinning. "Hey, Little Charlie, get a couple of guys to pull that diesel engine out of the fire truck, then haul the engine to shore and take it over to the dock. Get a crew to take the saltwater pump off the truck and haul it up to the fire station. Get the jacks from the storage shed while you're there. I put them out last night. We'll anchor the jacks on logs next to the back tires, lift the truck once it's lighter and then winch it up onto the beach."

Crews were rushing and working, doing exactly what Big Charlie said but starting before Big Charlie had a chance to yell out his orders. Everyone already knew what to do.

"You can save everything?" asked Curtis Vandermeulen.

"Sure. No problem," answered Big Charlie, patting his Member of Parliament on the back.

"And you can put it all back together?"

"Well," said Big Charlie slowly. "I suppose we could if we wanted. But it's not really worth the effort. I mean, I think we should just mount the pump on wheels so we can roll it close to any fire. Let's both forget about putting that pump back on the truck. I mean, we don't really need a truck. Besides, a big fire truck like this one is going to take up a lot of room in that garage. I have to admit that the fire truck is even bigger than I thought it would be. We need the garage space for storage."

"But the fire truck?"

"Don't worry," said Big Charlie, slapping Mr. Vandermeulen on the back again. "It'll be fine."

"Fine."

"Sure. The kids are going to love it."

"The kids?"

"We'll name the park after you."

"The park?"

"The park on the sandy road where we're going to put the fire engine. Kids can climb all over it. I wrote you a letter once about playground equipment. Your assistant wrote back that the federal government isn't responsible for playgrounds."

Little Charlie raced past the two men, holding a jack in one hand.

"I don't understand," said Mr. Vandermeulen slowly.

"Actually," said Big Charlie, pulling an apple out of his jacket pocket and taking a bite, "I think maybe you're beginning to."

"You never intended to…"

"Oh, sure, we intended to accept the

fire engine, but how could we have anticipated that it would get stuck and that we would have to strip it down fast, before the tide rolls in and the salt-water ruins the entire truck. And, once the truck is light enough to be pulled up onto the beach, why should we put the engine—which we own—back into the fire engine. Annie Pritchard's boat needs a new engine. She's a national treasure, you know. Well, of course you know. She's about the most famous person up and down the entire coast. You helped nominate her for the Order of Canada, didn't you?"

"Yes, I did."

"And we were all mighty grateful. She's our treasure, too, and we don't want anything to happen to her. A new engine purring along inside her boat will make all of us feel a lot better. And since the fire truck can't move without an engine, we won't need all that space behind the second row of houses for a road. And since we don't need the road, we can put the fire truck behind the school and use it as a superb piece of playground equipment, something we've needed for a long time. And since the fire truck won't be kept in the garage, we can use the entire garage for storage space. Isn't it amazing how you've helped this small little village? We got a water pump, storage space, a sandy playground, playground equipment, an engine for Annie's boat and the saltwater pump I originally requested."

Big Charlie slapped the MP on the back, hard. "We'll certainly be voting for you in the next election."

6
ONE THUMB DECIDES TO LEAVE

FOUR days later Susan and I sat inside the fire truck. I was in the driver's seat, smiling, of course, and turning the steering wheel while I bounced up and down, pretending that the truck was moving quickly over a rough road.

"So you knew all about the plan?" asked Susan again, still surprised.

"I told you and Little Charlie told you, too. It was my plan."

"You planned on making the fire truck sink in the sand so we could justify tearing it apart?"

"Sort of. I said it was a shame we kids couldn't play on the fire truck and Dad and Little Charlie made up the rest."

"Do you think you should be smiling if we're supposed to be rushing to a fire?" asked Susan. "Shouldn't you be frowning, worried about the dangers we're about to face?"

"I am frowning," I said.

"No, you're not."

"Well, this is my frown."

"When people frown, the corners of their mouths are supposed to curl down. The corners of your mouth are curling up. That's a smile."

"I have a muscle deformity," I said, still concentrating on my driving, even though the fire truck was anchored in the sand behind the school and was certainly not moving. "The corners of my mouth can't curl down."

"Is that true?" asked Susan.

"I don't think so, but as long as we're pretending that this fire truck is moving and we're firefighters heading out to battle a big blaze, then we can pretend I have a muscle deformity that makes it look as if I'm always smiling. I'm too excited to frown. This is fun. Do you have any idea what all these buttons are supposed to do? I didn't know cars and trucks had so many buttons."

"I suppose a couple of them are for the radio."

"Do you think firefighters listen to the radio on their way to a blaze?" I asked. "I mean, if they're listening to a baseball game and the star hitter is coming up to bat, do they sit in the fire truck for a minute and listen after they get to the fire? Do they wait for a song to finish?"

"They probably aren't supposed to listen on the way to a fire," said Susan. "I bet they can only listen if they're taking the truck out to get gas or something. Maybe the radio is for listening for news about fires."

"Yeah," I said, still driving.

"Leon?"

"Yeah?"

"Did you hear that Little Charlie is leaving tomorrow?"

I stopped driving. I even took my foot off the gas pedal and pressed the brake. I yanked on the emergency brake and turned to look at Susan.

"Little Charlie is leaving?"

"Yeah."

"Just for a little while?"

"No. He has a construction job back east, in Ontario."

"But what about his thumb?"

"I suppose," said Susan slowly, "that both of Little Charlie's thumbs are going with him."

"He can't do that."

"Sure he can. His thumbs are attached, remember?"

I opened the truck door and hopped out, running toward Big Charlie's house. Susan ran after me, shouting, "Wait! Little Charlie's not home. He's at the gym."

I swung open the gym door. The lights were on and the bleachers on one side of the basketball court were full. I stood in the doorway, stunned.

Nobody clapped or said a word. Dad walked over and led me to the center of the gym floor where Big Charlie and Little Charlie and Annie Pritchard were standing, watching us.

I didn't know what was happening, but I knew it was about me and I knew it was important and I started to blush.

I turned toward the door. Susan was leaning against the side of the door, smiling at me.

We stopped at the center court circle and Dad took a step backwards.

"As you all know," said Big Charlie in his loudest voice, "my son is leaving us. We don't know when he'll be back. While he is gone, New Auckland is going to have visitors. We always do. Fishermen. People sailing their small boats up and down the coast. School board officials here on inspection tours.

Art critics, here to stare at our basketball court jump circle.

"We'd like to play the thumb joke on these people," said Big Charlie, looking straight at me as he put a huge hand on my shoulder. "But Little Charlie's thumbs are going with him. So, Leon, we had a meeting and decided that you are going to have an accident, and one of your thumbs is going to be severed clean off. Fortunately, the doctors down in Vancouver are going to put it back on for you, with tiny screws to hold it in place."

I knew that Big Charlie didn't mean I was really going to lose a thumb.

"Now, don't get all big-headed and think this is some terrific honor," said Big Charlie. "It isn't. We were going to pick Mrs. Yatulis, but she can't lie. So we looked around for the best darned liar in the village and decided that your smile makes it impossible for anybody to know when you're lying. Now, Leon, it's your turn to say something."

"I don't know what to say."

"Good," said Big Charlie quickly, "because I can hear the plane landing and I don't want Little Charlie to miss it. It is my duty as mayor to present you with this box that Annie Pritchard carved for the occasion."

Big Charlie took a step forward, reached into his coat pocket and pulled out a small white cardboard box tied with a red ribbon. I untied the ribbon, took off the lid and looked inside. A wooden box lay nested in white tissue paper. A large bird was carved on the top of the wooden box, both eyes staring up at me.

"It's a raven," said Annie. "Ravens are tricksters. They play practical jokes and watch practical jokes and laugh a lot, mostly at people. It seemed right to carve a raven on the lid."

◆

This whole story took place thirty-two years ago. I still own that wooden box. It is my most prized possession. Every summer I go back to New Auckland, and I tell any of the children now old enough all about my severed thumb. I show them my thumb after making them watch me work, all day, to make sure my thumb doesn't fly off while I repaint the fire truck a bright, sparkling red.